R.L. STINE

GIVE YOURSELF

Goosebumps®

ZOMBIE SCHOOL

AN
APPLE
PAPERBACK

SCHOLASTIC INC.
New York Toronto London Auckland Sydney
Mexico City New Delhi Hong Kong

A PARACHUTE PRESS BOOK

ISBN 0-590-99397-6

12 11 10 9 8 7 6 5 4 3 2 1

9/9 0 1 2 3 4/0

Printed in the U.S.A.

40

First Scholastic printing, November 1999

Standing in the doorway is a student about your age. But he looks totally weird! His skin is bluish-green. His eyes are unfocused, as if he's staring at something a million miles away. His arms hang slack at his sides.

Whoa! you think. What's wrong with him?

He shuffles forward. Then he mumbles, "It's good to obey the rules." His ragged voice makes your skin crawl.

"He — he looks like a zombie!" the kid beside you whispers.

He sure does, you think. What's going on here?

Wait a minute! This must be some kind of a new student joke. This guy's not for real. Ha! They didn't fool you!

"This is what happens to bad students," Miss Simms threatens. "Think about that. I'll be back in a minute."

She leads the "zombie" out of the room.

You chuckle. Time to show everyone what a joke this whole thing is! You stride to the teacher's desk.

"Well, class," you say, imitating Miss Simms's voice. "Does anyone want to break the rules now?"

A few kids laugh. You put Miss Simms's monocle in one eye.

Yikes! What you see through it stops you cold!

Grab hold of PAGE 5.

RANEWASH BOARDING SCHOOL IS *BRAINWASH* BOARDING SCHOOL, the paper reads.

"Hah!" You snort. That's a good one.

You head toward homeroom. The classroom isn't far, and soon you're settled into a desk.

You glance at your homeroom teacher. Totally weird-looking, you decide. She has a pinched face and long red fingernails. And — really strange — she's wearing a monocle in one eye!

"I am Miss Simms. Welcome to Ranewash Boarding School," she begins. "A place where rules are very important.

"If you disobey the rules, you will get demerits," she continues. "And any student who reaches twenty-five demerits will wind up in the *Detention Wing*!"

Something about the way Miss Simms says the words sends a chill up your spine.

What happens in the Detention Wing? you wonder.

As if she can read your mind, the teacher explains, "In the Detention Wing, we make examples out of bad students. Maybe you'd like to see one of our examples. . . ."

Miss Simms points at the door.

It opens and you all gasp.

Open to PAGE 4.

BEWARE!!
DO NOT READ THIS
BOOK FROM
BEGINNING TO END!

You are totally happy as you settle into your new school, Ranewash Boarding School. Only the best students go here, and you're sure to meet the kids of lots of famous people — actors, athletes, even astronauts!

But Ranewash isn't all it appears to be. Soon you realize that the teachers at the school are brainwashing the kids! And you have to escape before you're next! But how?

Maybe you should team up with the girl next to you, who seems just as freaked out as you are. But how can you be sure she's not another brain-washed zombie? You could try sneaking out as part of a class trip — but what will happen if you get caught?

This scary adventure is all about you. You decide what will happen. And you decide how terri-fying the scares will be!

Start on *PAGE 1*. Then follow the instructions at the bottom of each page. You make the choices. If you choose well, you'll make it home again. But if you make the wrong choice ... BEWARE!

SO TAKE A DEEP BREATH. CROSS YOUR FINGERS. AND TURN TO *PAGE 1* TO *GIVE YOURSELF GOOSEBUMPS*!

READER BEWARE —
YOU CHOOSE THE SCARE!

Look for more
GIVE YOURSELF GOOSEBUMPS adventures
from R.L. STINE:

The classroom looks completely different!

The chalkboards that were empty a second ago are now covered with the words OBEY WITHOUT QUESTION and WORK, DON'T PLAY.

Your eyes fall on an open book on your teacher's desk. Through one eye, it seems like a normal textbook. But through the monocle lens, you see the same words over and over again: *Never question authority.*

You glance at the other students. Some are smiling, waiting for your next joke. But some of them look different through the monocle! Their eyes are glassy. Their skin is greenish-blue.

Hey! you think. They look like the zombie kid!

And they have big red numbers on their clothes.

Like on prison uniforms! you realize.

What exactly is going on in this place?

Then you hear footsteps. Miss Simms is coming back! You have to get back to your seat!

Maybe if you keep the monocle, you can use it to find out what's going on. But what if you get caught with it? Maybe you should just put it back.

To keep the monocle, go to PAGE 58.
To put the monocle back, go to PAGE 93.

6

You decide to mind your own business. You go back to your chair, trying to ignore the pain.

But you can't! Your head pounds like someone's beating it with a baseball bat. Oh, no! you think. You *have* to be a spy!

You can't stand it anymore!

You try to find the two students again. But the pain is so intense you can't even see.

Uh-oh! you think. You waited too long!

As your vision grows dark, you wonder if your head really *will* explode. It sure feels like it will.

Which makes this the most horrible . . .

END.

The police car rumbles up the drive. A smiling officer wearing sunglasses gets out. He walks up to you.

"You're the student who called?" he asks.

"Yes," you answer. "You see, I found this monocle, and I saw these —"

"That's enough," he snaps, and takes out a pair of handcuffs.

"What's going on?" you cry.

He ignores you and slaps them on your wrists.

Then you see the Ranewash Boarding School ring on his finger.

I'm doomed! you realize. He's a graduate of Ranewash!

He pulls off his sunglasses and glares at you.

The bad news is you're headed to jail — for a *long* time.

The good news is that by the time you get out of jail, you won't have to deal with Ranewash anymore.

Because you'll be way too old for school by then!

THE END

The big guards drag you and Kate into the room with Dr. Ranewash and the teachers.

"Stop! Why are you doing this to us?" Kate screams.

"Only the best students come to Ranewash Boarding School," Dr. Ranewash says. "Students who will be powerful leaders as adults. Soon all the most important people in the world will obey me!"

You gulp as you remember some of the famous people who went to Ranewash: scientists, politicians, athletes, movie stars, judges. All of them must be obeying Dr. Ranewash! Doing whatever he says.

If he keeps it up, Dr. Ranewash really will control the world!

He has to be stopped! But what can you do?

Concentrate! you order yourself. There *must* be a way out of this. But what is it?

Though you're not sure why, your mind flashes back to the Brainwash Chairs you saw upstairs. You remember the warning label ... SUBJECT MUST NOT WEAR ANY METAL!

Are you wearing anything made of metal?

Check what you're wearing now. A belt buckle? A ring? Braces? Is there a paper clip or a coin in your pocket?

If you're wearing any metal, turn to PAGE 98.
If not, turn to PAGE 54.

Hopefully no one will notice as you slip through the fire exit.

RRRRRRRRING! The piercing sound fills the assembly hall. You set off the alarm on the door! Suddenly everyone in the assembly hall is staring right at you.

You slap your forehead with your hand. You might as well have jumped up and down, shouting, "Here I am!"

You shove through the door and burst outside.

You notice a broom leaning against the outside wall. Yes! You shove it through the handles of the double doors behind you. That should keep anyone from following you for a little while.

But where do you go now?

You could run into the forest outside the school. Then again, remember those red eyes you saw from the bus? Who knows what might be lurking among those trees?

To your left is the soccer field. You can see the highway on the other side of it. That might be the safer choice, but what if the broomstick gives way? There's nowhere to hide in an open field!

Which way should you run?

To head into the forest, turn to PAGE 56.
To run across the soccer field, turn to PAGE 86.

10

You head toward the assembly hall. Kate follows close behind you. You sneak past the closed classroom doors in silence. You can't speak — not if you want to make it out of there.

Kate gasps softly behind you. She's staring through the monocle at the messages hidden in the wall murals. She must be as amazed as you were when you first saw them.

Then you hear a growl. It's coming from somewhere in front of you.

No! You flatten yourself against a row of lockers. Kate crouches next to you.

Your heart pounds. Something just around the corner casts an ominous shadow into the hall. A sound like a huge animal's panting fills your ears.

You remember the red eyes of the beast you spotted from the bus. Could this be a creature like that?

You try to turn and run, but your feet feel like they weigh a thousand pounds each.

You only manage to utter one strangled word to Kate.

"Dog," you croak.

The panting grows closer. . . .

Turn to PAGE 51.

There's another voice on the line.

And it sounds *exactly* like *your* voice!

"Just tell Mom and Dad that I'm having a great time, okay?" the voice says.

"Maggie, don't listen to that!" you interrupt. "That's not me!" But somehow, Maggie can't hear you anymore.

"Okay," Maggie answers. "You *must* be having a great time to call after you've only been gone for two hours."

"Maggie!" you shout. "Tell them to come get me!"

The voice that sounds like yours speaks again. "That's all, Maggie. Just remember, if you work hard, you might get to come to Ranewash too. Work is better than play."

"Yeah, what*ever*," Maggie mutters. "Bye."

"Bye," the voice answers. You hear the click of your sister hanging up.

"No!" you shout. Someone must have been listening in.

They must know who you are! you realize.

You're doomed!

You hear your voice on the phone again.

"Do you have a hall pass, young man?" it asks.

Maybe not, but you do have a pass to PAGE 71.

The door closes with a snap.

Before you is a forest. The one the bus drove through earlier. The one where you first saw that huge dog with its gleaming red eyes. *Gulp.*

The trees are so dense that you can only see a few yards in front of you. You hold the hall pass tighter as you enter the dark woods.

You crash through the underbrush, following the map.

Your throat tightens as you hear a low growl. Panicked, you glance around. Behind you a huge, dark shadow moves through the trees.

Oh, no! Not again! You start to run.

But wait a minute. What are you worried about? You've still got the hall pass. Right?

You stare down into your hands.

Noooo! You've still got the map, but no hall pass! You must have dropped it! And now *something* is stalking you.

Maybe you should just follow the map as fast as you can toward the Runaways. But you don't want to meet up with a dog without that hall pass! Maybe you should search for it first.

To follow the map, go to PAGE 97.
To search for the hall pass, turn to PAGE 84.

You're off to English class.

The teacher tells you all to find partners. You look carefully at the girl sitting next to you. What if she is one of the zombies?

You wish you could take a quick look through the monocle. But if the teacher saw it, you'd be in trouble.

"Want to be my partner?" you offer.

"Okay," she answers, peering back at you suspiciously. Maybe she's also noticed that things here at Ranewash are a little weird, you think.

"I'm Kate," she mutters. "Is this your first year?"

You nod. She looks relieved. "Mine too," she tells you.

The teacher hands out the assignment sheets. You and Kate have to write an essay or story together. The suggested themes are: "How you could be injured while playing" and "What bad things happened the last time you disobeyed?"

"Great topics," Kate mutters with a smirk.

"Maybe we could think of a better one," you suggest.

"I've got a really interesting idea for a story," Kate tells you.

What's the idea? Find out on PAGE 132.

14

You decide to join the field trip. After all, once everyone gets off that bus it could go straight back to school!

You follow the other students, trying to look brain-dead. You glance up at the sign on the building in front of you: RANEWASH GENERAL HOSPITAL.

Well, *that* doesn't give you a good feeling. A guide takes your group through the hospital, pointing out areas with names like Radiology and Intensive Care.

Soon, your group arrives at a door labeled OR-GAN TRANSPLANTS.

"When people's organs become diseased, we can transplant other people's organs into their bodies," the guide explains. "But where can we get fresh new organs?" He pauses. "Just lie on these beds and you'll find out."

What? you think. Is this guy about to do what you think he's going to do? Is he about to steal your organs?

You're not sticking around to find out! You start to back out of the door, hoping no one will notice you.

Then someone grabs your arm. Before you can turn around, you feel a sting on your arm. Your skin tingles. And you start to feel very sleepy!

Transplant yourself to PAGE 62.

You decide to head for the assembly hall. You'll bide your time and look for a way out.

You get there just as the bell rings. The assembly hall seems crowded with all the students in school. Everyone is in lines, waiting to sign up for classes.

You get in line for a class. Any class!

You sweep your eyes across the assembly hall.

Uh-oh! Miss Simms! She's across the room, gingerly holding her monocle with a handkerchief. That's the monocle with *your* fingerprint on it.

She's staring right at you! And now she's coming your way!

You nervously scan the room for an exit. Run!

You duck out of the line and try to lose her in the crowd.

Yes! There's a fire exit right in front of you.

Take the exit to PAGE 9.

You decide to go through Entrance 17.

"Okay," you murmur. "After you . . ."

Kate slowly pushes open the door. Red light spills from the entrance. You follow her inside, onto a narrow staircase. Your footsteps echo against the metal stairs as you move farther and farther down.

Finally, you reach an open doorway. The sound of voices comes from the other side. You and Kate creep up to the door and peer through.

A very old man sits at a large metal table. Sitting with him are some of the Ranewash teachers.

The old man talks softly. You strain to hear his words. "In the old days programming students took years," he mumbles. "Recently we've gotten the same results in a week. Imagine — in just one week all these children will be our slaves — forever!"

Turn to PAGE 134.

Through the monocle the video shows students at Ranewash Boarding School as they grow up, graduate, and get jobs in the outside world.

The scary thing is that they all have that brainwashed look. Like the "zombie" in homeroom. And even scarier, these aren't just ordinary people. They are politicians, actors, heads of huge businesses. . . .

Oh, no! you think. Ranewash graduates run everything! And they're all zombies!

The hidden layer of the video ends with a message for all Ranewash graduates. . . .

WE NEVER FORGET OUR SCHOOL!

The teacher flicks the light back on and stands. You quickly shove the monocle back into your pocket.

You don't know what's going on here — but you know you don't like it.

"Now we'll make sure you were all paying attention. Time for an oral quiz! I hope you were watching carefully, because anyone failing the test gets fifteen demerits!"

Oh, no! You were watching carefully, all right. But you were watching the wrong thing! You remember what Miss Simms said in homeroom. Twenty-five demerits and you go to the Detention Wing!

Turn to PAGE 55.

The two scents are mixing together.

And they're turning *purple*.

Oh, no! you think. Red and blue make purple, and that's the color that makes the dogs attack!

A long growl confirms your suspicions. The dogs are moving closer, looking angrier with every step.

They're about to pounce!

You try to spray more blue scent on you, but the dogs can't resist someone with even a whiff of purple scent on them.

You always thought this plan stunk.

And you were right in . . .

THE END.

You frantically dial 911 for the police.

They answer after only one ring.

"I'm a student at Ranewash Boarding School," you explain quickly. "There's something strange going on here. There are hidden messages everywhere, and I think some of the students have been *brainwashed* somehow!"

You can't believe you're saying this. It all sounds so *crazy*. But they *have* to believe you!

"Slow down," the officer on the other end tells you. "I've thought for a long time there was something funny about that school. Maybe you and I should have a talk."

Yes! you think. He believes you!

"Meet me at the front entrance," the officer instructs. "But don't tell *anyone* what you just told me."

"Okay," you agree, and hang up the phone.

You sneak to the front entrance through the now-empty halls. You open the big front door as quietly as you can.

A few minutes later a police car comes down the drive.

Yes! You're saved!

Turn to PAGE 7.

It's a *stamp* tax! The answer must be —
"Stamps!" you proclaim.

The teacher scowls. Uh-oh! You're wrong!

The teacher shakes his head. "Fifteen demerits. And remember what happens if you get twenty-five? The Detention Wing!"

He takes your class schedule and writes *fifteen demerits* on it with a big red pen.

Gulp! You remember the "example" kid you were shown in homeroom. You don't want to go to the Detention Wing!

Then the bell rings and class is over.

The question is, did you already have some demerits from other classes?

Total your demerits. If they add up to twenty-five demerits or more, go to the Detention Wing on PAGE 28.

If they add up to less than twenty-five demerits, write down fifteen demerits *and go to your next class. If you have forgotten the room number, check the list on PAGE 60.*

Your hands are starting to slip! You can't seem to hold on any longer. But then you think back to the last time you fell off a jungle gym.

Ouch! Did that hurt! *This* would be ten times worse!

That settles it, you are *not* going to fall. You are not going to "wash out"!

You grit your teeth and reach for every last ounce of energy you've got. Hand over hand, you pull yourself all the way to the other end.

Sweat runs into your eyes, blinding you. But your aching hands manage to find the rope ladder. You grab it and climb down.

You made it!

"Yes!" you shout. You give a thumbs-up to the next student. But the coach grabs your shoulder.

"We'll see if you're so tough tomorrow," he growls. "We'll be running through our obstacle course — called 'the Exterminator'!"

Oh sure, you think. Can't wait for that — not! You head to the locker room to change. You are out of here!

Go to the next class on your schedule. If you forgot the room number, check the list on PAGE 60.

You decide to choose the green bottle.

Ally sprays you both with the scent in the blue bottle — the one for making hall passes. She saves the green bottle for when you meet the dogs.

You head back through the woods toward the school.

Soon you see glowing red pairs of eyes gathering around you. You hear the panting of the monstrous dogs as they stalk you through the forest. You start to tremble as you emerge into a clearing close to the school.

Who voted for this crazy idea? you wonder.

Oh, yeah. You did.

The huge beasts step out into the open, baring their teeth and growling. But when Ally holds out her hand, one sniffs it and backs away.

They're not attacking! The scent in the blue bottle works!

Then Ally turns to you and sprays you with green bottle.

The dogs' ears perk up, and they start to crowd in around you. They move in so close that you can feel their hot breath on your hands. A strangled cry of fear escapes your lips.

What's happening? Are they going to attack?

Find out on PAGE 76.

You wait until the teacher isn't looking. Then you reach over and dip a brush in the "red" paint can. You try a few dabs on the mural. They're invisible, until you peer at them through the monocle!

Yes! It looks like your idea could work. . . .

What if you painted your own slogan onto the mural?

You could write whatever you want, and no one would see it. But just like the other hidden messages, maybe it would change the way people around here think.

You could write LET US GO HOME! Or, PLAY IS FUN!

After all, you've got to do *something*. You can't just wait around until *you* wind up brainwashed!

Of course, if a teacher saw your message with a monocle, they'd know someone was up to something.

And if you get caught, you'll probably be in a whole lot of trouble. You remember homeroom. The "example" student who'd been to the Detention Wing.

Gulp. You don't want to wind up like *that*!

Should you risk it?

To paint your own invisible slogan, go to PAGE 31.

To forget the whole idea, go to PAGE 130.

You wake up hearing Kate's voice.

"Get me out of here," comes her muffled cry.

You leap up, ready to obey. Obeying is good.

Hey. What was that weird thought? Oh, well. Whatever.

You release Kate from the chair. She glances around the room and you do the same. Everyone seems half asleep. Kate reaches for her mouth.

"My braces are killing me," she mutters.

Braces? you think. The warning you saw in the chair flashes into your head . . . no metal allowed!

Kate's braces must have made the chair malfunction!

"Give us orders," the others in the room plead.

"Yes, orders!" you agree. Weird. You never liked being ordered around before. But now you do — since that lightning bolt hit you.

Kate quickly gets used to ordering people around. She especially likes giving orders to you. One of her favorite things to ask you to do is get her ice cream sundaes. Which would be easy — if she didn't order you to make the ice cream from scratch. Starting with milking the cow.

Looks like getting hit by that jolt was a totally *moo*-ving experience.

THE END

You nod.

"I'll stay here during the next vacation," you decide. "And maybe even the one after that — to do lots and lots of work."

"Now, start on that letter," the teacher orders.

You click on the word-processing program. As you write your letter, you hear a funny sound, as if there's a voice screaming in your head. It's saying that you don't want to work all the time. That you *like* going on vacations.

But that doesn't make sense. Working is the best thing ever! Besides, the teacher told you to write this letter. And obeying is good.

Wow! With that attitude, we have a feeling you'll be obeying the teachers here at Ranewash Boarding School for a long time. And while you're following orders, obey this: Close this book, because you've reached

THE END.

You decide to blame Kate. After all, why should *you* get demerits for not going along with *her* essay idea?

You quickly explain about the essay she wanted to write. The teacher seems shocked, then he nods his head.

"Well, we'll have to put a stop to Kate's little tricks," he announces.

You gulp, feeling guilty already. You hope that nothing too bad happens to Kate.

"But we don't approve of tattlers here, either," the teacher snaps. "Ten demerits for snitching! And ten demerits for Kate as well!"

Whoa! You expected Kate to get some demerits. But you can't believe you got them too! That's totally unfair!

The question is, have you reached twenty-five demerits yet? If you have, you'll be taking a trip to the Detention Wing. . . .

Total your demerits. If they add up to twenty-five demerits or more, go to the Detention Wing on PAGE 28.

If they add up to less than twenty-five demerits, write down ten demerits *and go to your next class. If you have forgotten the room number, check the list on PAGE 60.*

At first Ranewash seems like a perfect town. There is no litter. There is no noise. The houses are all freshly painted.

The people are so well dressed, they look like models for a clothing catalog. Everything seems orderly and perfect. . . .

So perfect, it's creepy, you realize. Real life isn't this neat, and not everyone looks picture-perfect. There's only one explanation you can think of for this.

Maybe Ranewash town is filled with hidden messages — just like the school.

Which means you've got to get out of here!

At the end of the main street, you find a bus station. And there's a bus leaving for your town in an hour. You haven't got the fare, but maybe you could scrounge it up.

Then, across the street, you spot the local television station. Wow! Maybe inside you could broadcast a message to the world about Ranewash Boarding School. Then you'd not only save yourself but everyone else in the school!

Should you try to take the bus to your hometown?

Or should you try to broadcast a warning to the world?

To try to get bus fare, head for PAGE 82.
To try to broadcast a warning, go to PAGE 70.

DETENTION WING, reads the sign on the wall.

No! your mind screams. You remember the empty-eyed zombie student from the Detention Wing you saw in homeroom. Are you going to wind up like him?

You glance around. The room is full of nervous students.

"Sign in and sit down!" orders a uniformed guard. "You will be tested in the order you arrived."

Tested? you think. How? And on what?

You write your name in a big, musty book by the door. Whoa! You stare at the book. There must be *thousands* of names in here!

You sit in an empty chair.

One by one the students are called to be "tested." They disappear behind a big metal door at one end of the room. When the first student comes back out, he looks normal — not like a zombie at all. Whew! you think. Maybe this place isn't so bad after all.

But then the second student returns. Her face is now a ghastly bluish-green. Her eyes are completely empty.

Gulp! Maybe she failed the test!

The third student doesn't come out at all. . . .

Then the guard calls your name. Yikes! It's your turn!

Take your turn on PAGE 99.

You decide to turn in the two students.

You don't want to do it, but you can't take the pain!

Peering over their shoulders, you read their names from their class schedules. Then you head back to the Detention Wing. You give the names to Miss Pierce.

"I told you that you'd cooperate." She cackles cruelly.

You feel guilty at first. But suddenly an incredible feeling comes over you. It's as if your head is full of the most wonderful smells and tastes and sounds. Wow!

After a few minutes, you feel normal again.

"That was your reward," Miss Pierce explains. "Now go catch some more bad students."

"No way!" you insist.

But you can't help yourself. Every time you hear students grumble or complain, you just *have* to turn them in.

Hey! We can't resist asking, would you like some cheese? Because you turned into a real *rat* in . . .

THE END.

There's an emergency exit just past your room. You can beat the dogs to it, you decide.

You turn and bolt. The beasts howl, a terrible sound that makes your whole body quake.

You can see the emergency exit in front of you. You've almost made it!

"Nooo!" you yell. You feel a beast's teeth clamp onto your pant leg. It's got you!

You tumble to the floor. The monocle, the map, and the hall pass all fall from your grasp.

The three beasts crowd around you. Their teeth snap at your hands and feet.

*Dog*gone it, it looks like you've been beaten. Maybe you should take yourself out for a little walk — and try again another time.

THE END

You decide to risk it and paint your own slogan. Maybe you can beat *Brainwash* Boarding School at its own game!

You watch the teacher carefully. Once her back is turned, you jump into action.

You dip your brush into the invisible paint, then you reach out and paint the first thing that comes into your head — LET US GO HOME! — in huge letters.

And maybe you should write a message for your fellow students. Something to help them break out of zombie mode!

THINK FOR YOURSELF! you scrawl.

You put the monocle away and stare at your work.

Cool! It works! Just gazing at the painting makes you feel more in control — more alert.

But that feeling disappears when you hear the art teacher's voice.

"Nice work," she comments.

You gulp and turn around. Then, as you see her face, you suddenly remember. . . .

She's wearing glasses! Can she see what you've done through them?

Feast your eyes on PAGE 101.

Through the monocle, you see that the piece of paper has a secret message. *You found a special lens*, it reads. *Good work! Welcome to the Runaways.*

Whoa. You swallow nervously as you keep reading.

Join us! Follow the map on the other side of this piece of paper. It leads to our secret hideout.

Join them? Hmmm.

You turn the paper over. Sure enough, you see a map of the school and grounds, and a message: *Use the hall pass hidden in the crack to get through the halls.*

You fish around in the hole where you found the note. You find an old, crumpled piece of paper labeled HALL PASS.

Okay — you're going, you decide. The map shows the way.

You steal into the hall, keeping both eyes out for the hall monitor dog. You gasp! What's that noise?

You turn a corner — and find yourself face-to-face with a huge, angry dog.

Two shadows move behind it. Correction ... make that *three* huge, angry dogs.

Maybe you should use the hall pass. The note said it would get you through the hall safely. But dogs can't read, you reason. Shouldn't you be running like crazy?

To show the dog the hall pass, turn to PAGE 106.
To run like crazy, turn to PAGE 30.

Sweat rolls down your back as one student after another tries the Eliminator. It will be a while till they get to you, you realize.

"Aaaaaaah!"

You wince as another student is sucked from the pool down into the dark tunnel. You have to clench your teeth to keep from screaming with fear.

Please let this class be over soon! Please just let the bell ring! you think.

"You're next!" the coach shouts.

Oh, no! He's pointing at you!

You approach the rope ladder slowly. Your stomach twists with fear. Will you be able to survive the Eliminator?

Your fingers touch the ladder — and the bell rings!

Whew!

"We'll be starting with *you* next time," the coach grumbles, looking down at you with his burning eyes.

Oooh, great, you think. Can't wait.

Go to the next class on your schedule. If you have forgotten the room number, check the list on PAGE 60.

You raise your hand high. "I vote for Ally's plan," you say. "Let's try to take control of the dogs."

"Yes!" Ally cries.

"That's crazy," Max mutters. "*I'm* not going to be the one to test the scents with those maniac dogs!"

"Fine," Ally retorts, grabbing your arm. "*We'll* test them. Then the dogs will be in *our* power."

Wait a minute! You didn't volunteer for *that*!

Ally shows you the bottles containing the different scents.

"The teachers use this blue scent for making hall passes," she explains. "The dogs won't attack you if they smell it. We'll make sure we're wearing plenty! And we think the scent in this purple bottle makes the dogs attack. Be careful not to get any on you!"

Gulp. You take a step back from the purple bottle.

"Either the red or the green scent actually makes the dogs *obey* you," Ally continues. "But we don't know which one."

"Choose carefully," Max taunts. "Or you'll be dog food!"

Your eyes dart back and forth between the red and the green bottles. Which should you choose?

To try the red bottle, turn to PAGE 102.
To try the green bottle, turn to PAGE 22.

You tear off across the soccer field. You fix your eyes on the distant fence separating the field from the highway.

"On the soccer field! That way!" The shouts of teachers come from behind you.

No! They must have broken through the door!

You pump your legs even harder.

"Oh, no!" You groan as you reach the fence. It must be ten feet tall! And it's topped with awful barbed wire!

How are you going to get over it?

Maybe if you had a jacket, you could throw it over the wire to protect yourself.

Hmmm . . . are you wearing a jacket right now?

If you are wearing a jacket, turn to PAGE 47.
If not, turn to PAGE 83.

36

What you see makes your heart beat faster.

Hidden messages flash on your computer screen: OBEY WITHOUT THINKING. DON'T QUESTION AUTHORITY. WORK ALL THE TIME.

There are hundreds of the messages going by, and it feels as if they're zooming straight into your brain!

Oh, no! you think. This computer has been programming *you*! There must be some way you can turn off these messages.

You fiddle with a button on your monitor, and the messages seem to fade away. Whew! You decide it's safe to put away the monocle.

Now what? Maybe you should have a look at the school's database. It might help you find out what's going on here.

Or you could send an E-mail to your parents! You could tell them to come and get you out of this freaky place.

Hmmm. Which should you do?

To check out the school's database, click on PAGE 105.

To send an E-mail, click on PAGE 66.

I hate this school! you think quickly.

Whew! Well, looks like you're not brainwashed. You gasp when you see who has freed you.

It's Kate! She's not being held captive anymore.

You glance at Ranewash and the teachers who were sitting around the metal table. Everyone is totally still. Their hair is standing on end.

"The chair started freaking out," Kate explains. "Then it shot a big lightning bolt at the table. Everyone touching the table got zapped!"

"Are they — dead?" you ask.

"Not dead," one of them murmurs. "Ready to obey."

"Obeying is good," the others agree.

"Give us orders," Dr. Ranewash pleads. "Must obey."

"Cool!" Kate exclaims.

Yes! This turns out to be *very* cool. You're not sure how it happened, but now Ranewash and all the teachers have to obey *you*.

The first order you give is that everyone relax and have fun.

Best of all, you don't have to do any more homework.

But why should you? You are totally running Ranewash Boarding School now. And that's enough work for anyone!

THE END

You gulp as the teacher's eyes sweep the room. She's searching for a guilty face.

Just play it cool! you tell yourself.

RIIIING! You jump up as the bell goes off and head out the door with the other students.

The crowd swallows you up. "Ah," you sigh in relief. Miss Simms will never find you in the river of students headed to the assembly hall.

Then out of the corner of your eye you see a pay phone. Yes! you think. A link to the outside world!

You should call your parents and tell them what's going on. Then they'd come pick you up!

Or you could call the local police and tell them the weird stuff that's going on here. Then you'd be helping all the students at Ranewash.

But what if you're caught in the hall without a pass? You don't want to get any demerits. The Detention Wing isn't a joke anymore. Not after you saw that "example" kid.

What should you do?

To call your parents, dial PAGE 119.
To call the police, dial PAGE 19.
To head for the assembly hall, go on to PAGE 15.

You move toward the dark mouth of the cave.

A twig snaps under your foot.

The voices all stop.

You peer inside.

It's pitch-black! You can't see a thing!

A pair of strong hands shoot out from the cave.
They grasp your shoulders hard.

Aaaah! You're being pulled in!

Pull yourself to PAGE 89.

"Yes?" the teacher answers.

"It's kind of loud in here," Kate explains to the teacher. "May my partner and I work just outside the door?"

You let out your breath with a sigh. She's not turning you in after all.

The teacher nods his head. "But don't go anywhere without a hall pass," he warns.

Out in the hall, Kate whispers, "I've read about hidden messages like the ones you can see through the monocle. We've got to get out of here, or they'll wind up brainwashing us!"

The note you found in your room flashes into your mind ... *Ranewash Boarding School is* Brainwash *Boarding School.*

"I'm with you," you agree. "I don't want to wind up being a zombie."

"We'd better make a break for it," Kate whispers. She peers up and down the hall. "Which way should we go?"

You glance left and right. You realize you can either go toward the assembly hall or toward the front office.

Which will it be?

To go toward the assembly hall, turn to PAGE 10.
To go toward the front office, turn to PAGE 69.

You decide to follow their orders. If you can scare off the beast, maybe the Runaways will trust you. And *then* maybe they can help you get home.

Clutching the flare in your hand, you stride toward the mouth of the cave. The flare seems easy to use. The directions say to just rip the top off and the flare will light.

You peer out into the forest.

"Here, doggy-doggy!" you call, your voice cracking.

You don't see or hear a thing.

"Here —" you begin, but a sound cuts you off.

In front of you is the monstrous dog. It stares at you with its glowing red eyes. The beast's long, ugly tongue snakes out to lick its lips.

"Hu-hu-hungry?" you stammer, readying the flare.

The dog takes a few steps forward. You can't take your eyes off its fangs. Your hands shake as you clutch the flare.

It's about to leap!

"Come and fetch *this*!" you yell. You pull off the top of the flare.

And nothing happens. . . .

Go to PAGE 104.

"Billy?" Miss Simms points at a zombie student. "Who took my —"

RIIIIIING! The bell sounds.

"Oh, dear," the teacher mutters. "I didn't even have time to call the roll! And now you must all go to the assembly hall."

Whew! Saved by the bell!

The students head for the door — and you jump into the middle of the crowd. Roll was never even called, you reason. So no one even knows your name! You're safe. For now.

You head for the assembly hall. Crowds of students surge out of every classroom.

As you walk, you check out the rest of the school.

It seems normal enough, you think. Murals along the halls, drinking fountains, rows of lockers.

Maybe the stress of being in a new school is getting to you, you reason. Maybe you just imagined what you saw through the monocle. You slip it out of your pocket and sneak it into your eye for a quick glance around.

Take a peek on PAGE 107.

"T-tails," you stammer.

"It's heads," Dr. Ranewash says. "You lose." He smiles at Kate. "Which means *you* won. *You* go first."

"Thanks a lot," Kate mutters.

The burly guards drag Kate toward the chair. They lower the big helmet over her head.

You have to think of something fast!

"Throw the switch!" Ranewash orders. The guards obey and step back nervously.

The chair begins to whine. Kate's hands flex as if she's in terrible pain. You try to turn your eyes away, but you can't help watching. After all, you're next!

ZZZZZAP! Sparks appear on the helmet.

"What's going on?" Dr. Ranewash shouts.

The sparks dancing on the helmet grow larger and larger. Then a huge bolt of lightning shoots from the helmet to the metal table. It travels through the teachers seated there, then out to the guards. Finally it reaches you!

"Aaaah!" you shriek.

You crumple to the floor. . . .

See if you can crawl to PAGE 24.

44

I'll smash the bug! you decide. Anything to spoil this experiment.

You casually reach out for the device.

The teacher pauses. "Be very careful with that," she warns. "It has a very nasty antitampering system. . . ."

Her words choke off as you squeeze the little bug with all your strength.

"Oops!" you cry. But your mind shouts, *Yes!* The little device crumbles in your fingers.

Weird. The teacher doesn't seem upset at all.

She takes a step back from you. "It looks as if we're going to have a different sort of demonstration," she announces. "As I was saying, these bugs don't like it when you try to tamper with them. Observe."

She points the scalpel at your hand.

The skin between your fingers feels really tingly. You try to drop the remains of the bug, but you can't!

Hey! You can't move your hand at all!

See what's bugging you on PAGE 50.

"But I-I'm not a spy," you stammer. "I escaped from Ranewash Boarding School."

"We *all* escaped from Ranewash!" the voice shouts. "And they want us back. They're always sending spies like you to try to find us."

"But I'm just a student!" you exclaim. "I looked through this monocle and saw all these hidden messages, and —"

"You've seen the hidden messages? Maybe you *are* telling the truth," a voice interrupts.

They argue for a while, and finally decide to give you a test to see if you're a spy.

One of them thrusts a flare into your hand.

"Go and find the dog-beast and shove this flare in its face!" he orders.

"But — that's crazy!" you shout.

Should you follow their orders? Or run away from these crazy people?

To obey their orders, go to PAGE 41.
To run, turn to PAGE 80.

You remind yourself that Miss Pierce said this was a *logic* test, not a math test. Forget all that multiplication!

"There are only four feet in the mill," you answer. "The cats don't have feet. They have paws!"

"You're right!" Miss Pierce grumbles. She seems disappointed.

Whew! You passed! Now you won't get turned into a zombie.

"You're smarter than you look," she admits. "Smart enough to be useful. Take this book and go in there." Miss Pierce points at a door.

Uh-oh, you think. *That's* not the door you came in! You glance at the book she gave you.

Ancient Greek History, the cover reads.

You shrug and go through the door into a room.

It's full of students reading intently. That's funny. They all seem to be wearing weird hats.

You sit, open the book, and pretend to read.

Out of the corner of your eye, you peek at the student next to you.

Wait a minute! you think. She's not wearing a hat!

Aaaaaagh! It's some kind of *tentacle* on her head!

Head to PAGE 133.

You drag yourself painfully up the fence. Finally you reach the glistening barbed wire. You throw your jacket over it.

All right! The jacket protects you from the barbs.

You climb over the fence and drop to the ground. You glance back. The teachers are still after you!

Yes! Right in front of you is a bus stop, you realize. And pulling up to it is a local bus!

You wave your arms like crazy. The bus stops, and the door opens with a swishing sound.

You bolt up to the door.

"Hold it!" the driver barks. You stop short.

"Seventy-five cents," he announces.

"What?" you answer breathlessly.

"Seventy-five cents to ride the bus," he repeats.

You gulp and thrust your hands into your pockets.

Have you got any change?

Flip a coin.

If it's heads, you have seventy-five cents. Go to PAGE 108.

Tails, you don't have seventy-five cents. Go to PAGE 78.

"Uh . . . but I . . ." you stammer.

"Yes, you'll do nicely," the teacher interrupts. "Come up here right now."

You look around frantically. Is there a way for you to get out of here? The only door is right next to the teacher's desk. You're trapped.

You shuffle nervously to the front of the class.

The teacher takes your arm and stretches it out on the table. "First a little rubbing alcohol and anesthetic."

She dampens a cotton ball with something from a brown glass bottle. Whatever was in that bottle feels cold! A numbness creeps into your skin.

Your eyes widen as she picks up the scalpel.

Yikes! You've got to do something now, or you'll be stuck with a bug in your arm. Then these freaky teachers will always know where you are! And *that* can't be good!

Should you make a break for the door? It's only a few steps away.

Or maybe you could "accidentally" break the bug and ruin the experiment?

To make a run for it, turn to PAGE 126.
To squash that bug, go to PAGE 44.

You decide to play it cool. After all, Kate might be a spy for the school.

"Maybe we should write an essay about . . . um," you stammer, trying to remember the suggested topics, "the consequences of disobeying."

Kate rolls her eyes. "I can't think of anything more *boring*!"

Her hand shoots into the air.

"Yes?" the teacher asks.

"Can I change partners?" Kate asks.

The teacher peers at you suspiciously.

Gulp! Your heart starts to pound as everyone in the classroom stares right at you.

"Well, if your partner isn't cooperating, maybe you two should both work alone," the teacher decides.

You nod your head with a smile frozen on your face.

"And I'll see *you* after class," the teacher tells you.

You gulp. Maybe you should have been more cooperative.

Go to PAGE 110.

"What's happening?" you shout.

RIIIIP! Black tendrils that look like worms sprout out from between your fingers. They crawl up your arm and squeeze!

"Owww!" you howl in pain.

"Isn't today's technology wonderful, class?" the teacher explains. "The bug senses that it was damaged, so it will make sure that its host cannot escape. Let's watch what happens."

The wormlike tendrils reach your shoulder and start to wrap themselves around your neck. You claw at them with your other hand, but their grip tightens with crushing force.

You can't breathe!

Your vision starts to dim, but you can still hear the teacher's calm voice.

"You might say," she jokes, "that these bugs bite back!"

You try to speak, but all that comes out is a strangled croak.

Wow! Science class always bugged you — but this is ridiculous!

THE END

Whoa! Kate grabs your arm. She yanks you backwards through a door.

It's dark. You can't see a thing!

"Where —?" you start.

"Shhh!" she hisses. "We're in a janitor's closet."

The sound of the huge dog's feet padding down the hall silences you both. You hear it snuffling outside.

You imagine the beast's hot breath snaking under the door and surrounding your feet. Your toes curl up with fear inside your sneakers.

After a few moments the dog moves on, padding away until you can't hear it anymore.

Whew! You're safe . . . for now.

"Try to find the light," Kate whispers. You hear her fumbling in the dark for a switch.

Your reach out your hands. Your fingers close on something that feels like a light switch. You flick it.

But when the lights come on, you almost wish you'd stayed in the dark. . . .

Shed some light on PAGE 100.

"It's a *lot* of feet!" you tell Miss Pierce. "I mean, it's got to be at least ninety —"

"Wrong!" Miss Pierce cuts you off. "There are only four feet in the mill. The cats have *paws!*"

Oh, no! You blew it! Get ready to become a zombie!

The old woman cackles. She pushes a button on her desk.

Ahhh! What's happening? Your chair tilts back. Metal cuffs clamp over your wrists. Robot hands sprout from the back of the chair. They grab your head and point it upward.

You see a huge TV on the ceiling. Words race by on the screen. Crazy slogans like FIND THE BAD STUDENTS! and STUDENT SPIES ARE COOL! fill your mind.

No! You're being brainwashed! You clamp your eyes shut.

But the robot-chair's fingers pry your eyelids apart!

You *have* to watch! The slogans swirl through your head. Finally, the chair releases you.

Owww! What a headache! But for some reason, you don't *feel* like a zombie. . . .

"Well, back to class," Miss Pierce orders. "To start your new job."

"Job?" you echo.

"Spying," she answers. "So we can catch other bad students before they break the rules."

Spy your way to PAGE 79.

The teacher stomps toward the back. She stops at Kate's seat. She glares at Kate through her monocle.

"Where's your field trip pass?"

"Uh, I l-lost it?" Kate stammers.

"Lost it?" the teacher shrieks. "That's twenty-five demerits. Report to the Detention Wing immediately."

Uh-oh. The Detention Wing? That doesn't sound good!

The teacher doesn't see you, so you stay crouched as the bus pulls away. You glance back only when she sits down. You spot Kate darting into the forest instead of going back to school. Good luck, Kate, you think.

The bus takes a long, winding road. Everyone sits in total silence. At your old school everyone would be talking and having fun right now. Not these zombies. Yuck!

Finally the bus stops. The students file off.

All right, you think. There are two ways to handle this. You could follow everyone off the bus, or you could stay *on* the bus and make your escape when everyone's gone.

Which will it be?

To join the field trip, turn to PAGE 14.
To stay on the bus, turn to PAGE 116.

"You first!" Dr. Ranewash shouts.

Yikes! He's pointing at you! At least you're not wearing anything made of metal. You have a feeling it would be bad news if you were.

They drag you to the chair and strap you in.

The chair begins to hum. You feel electrical currents running across your forehead. It's as if bugs are running around in your hair.

It tickles so much, it's driving you crazy! You strain against the straps. If you could only reach up and pull the helmet from your head. . . .

But you can't move a muscle.

And there's a funny feeling in your head, as if everything were draining out of it bit by bit. . . .

At first you don't like the feeling. But after a while it doesn't matter so much.

You just wish that someone would tell you what to do.

Because obeying is good!

Uh-oh. Here's an order for you. Turn to PAGE 95.

The teacher walks around the room, asking each student one question about the American Revolution. Everyone answers correctly.

Finally, he gets around to you.

"So, what should I ask you?" he ponders. "Maybe a question about taxation."

He rubs his bald head in thought. "Name the most important item that was taxed by the British in the Stamp Act of 1765."

You rack your brain, but all you can remember is "No taxation without representation."

But what were they taxing?

How about wigs? All those guys wore powdered wigs during the Revolution. Or maybe it was tea? Everyone liked tea. Then again, maybe the Stamp Tax was a tax on stamps! That seems logical. But you're not sure.

If you think the answer is "wigs," turn to PAGE 73.

If you think the answer is "tea," turn to PAGE 115.

If you think the answer is "stamps," turn to PAGE 20.

You decide to run into the forest. It's the quickest way to disappear.

You plunge into the dense underbrush. Chills run up your spine as you remember the red eyes you saw from the bus. But you can't think about that now!

You crash through the forest. Branches whip your face and arms.

"In the forest! This way!" voices shout behind you.

Yikes! The broom you stuck through the door handles must have given way. The Ranewash teachers are on your trail!

You weave through the trees, and the voices fade into the distance.

All right! you think. They must have given up! You let yourself slow down a bit.

You glance around, trying to remember which way is which.

Wait a minute, where *are* you? Your heart pounds. In the chase you've lost your sense of direction.

You don't have a clue where you are!

Then you hear a sound that makes your hair stand on end. . . .

Turn to PAGE 59.

Owww! It feels like a bee stung you in the eye!

You grasp your face and fall to the ground. You hear the screams of your fellow Runaways around you. Strong hands grip you and drag you inside the Detention Wing.

When you can see again, you find yourself chained to the wall. What's even worse, you have to face the laughter of your captor.

Oh, no! you realize. It's Max! He's a Ranewash spy!

"Thanks for voting for my plan," he taunts you. "Before you came along, I couldn't get everyone to agree. Now, I've captured all the Runaways in one fell swoop."

Good move. Now you're stuck in detention — forever.

Which makes this your worst first day of school in history!

THE END

You decide to keep the monocle. There's more going on here than meets the naked eye! And the monocle might be the only way to find out what it is.

You slip it into your pocket and sprint to your desk. Miss Simms enters just as you reach your seat.

She explains that all classes will head to the assembly hall soon. But first she'll call the roll.

She peers for a moment at her desk, puzzled, as if looking for something.

"Did anyone see my monocle?" she asks.

You sure hope no one tells on you.

But as you watch in horror, a dozen students raise their hands.

And you realize they're the ones who looked like zombies through the monocle!

Gulp. Looks like you're in trouble. . . .

Get turned in on PAGE 42.

Howwwwwl!

Far off in the distance, you hear the cry of a beast. Something immense — and wolflike.

The howl sounds again. . . .

No! This time it's closer!

"Don't panic. Don't panic," you whisper to yourself. Now you know why your pursuers gave up so easily. Only a crazy person would come into these woods. Because there's something horrible living in here!

Your mind flashes back to that huge dog you saw from the bus on your way to Ranewash. The one with the glowing red eyes!

The beast howls again. You have to get out of here. You have to run. But how do you know where the thing is?

Hey! What if you went vertical? What if you climbed a tree? Maybe the howling thing is a wolf — and wolves can't climb — right?

To run away from the animal, get to PAGE 63.
To climb a tree, turn to PAGE 127.

You turn around. The voice belongs to a student. You catch a glimpse of him through the monocle before you cram it back in your pocket.

His skin is normal-colored. Not blue. Whew! That makes you feel better. Those zombie students creep you out!

"Ummm, nothing," you stammer. "Just this thing I found on the floor."

He shrugs and turns away.

You peer around the assembly hall and see a big sign that says CLASS SELECTION. There are sign-up tables all along the walls. Someone hands you a class selection form.

Well, you guess you'd better use it!

Pick your classes! Write down four of them in any order from the list below. Be sure to include the room numbers.

ART	Room 103
COMPUTING	Room 122
ENGLISH	Room 13
GYM	Room 77
HISTORY	Room 111
SCIENCE	Room 64

When you finish class selection, the bell rings.

Go to PAGE 135.

FWHOOSH!

Ow! A blinding light fills the cave!

The beast rears back, opening its mouth wide. In the bright light you can see its fangs, long and sharp and dripping with saliva.

It howls once, sending a shiver of panic down your spine. Then it turns and bounds out of the cave.

The light starts to dim a bit, leaving the image of the dog burned into your eyes. The hands release you.

Relieved laughter comes from behind you.

Dumbstruck, you turn around.

The cave is full of kids your age. A couple of them have Ranewash sweatshirts on.

"Those dogs may look tough," one of them announces. "But they're sure afraid of fire."

The others laugh. You notice that the first kid is holding a flare. He drops it to the ground and grinds it out with his foot. The light disappears again, returning the cave to darkness.

"The only question is," he continues, "what are we going to do with this spy?"

A couple of hands grab your arms again.

Spy?

Spy what happens next on PAGE 45.

The guide leads you to a bed. You try to fight him off. But you can't seem to move your arms. It's all you can do to keep from falling down.

"Don't worry," he murmurs soothingly. "You won't feel a thing."

You try to explain that you *need* your organs, but your mouth doesn't seem to work anymore.

Stop! your mind screams. But you can't say a word.

He puts you on the bed. No matter how hard you try, you can't move. In fact, you're falling asleep.

But maybe that's best.

You've got a feeling that you don't have the stomach for what's going to happen next.

Or the lungs. Or the heart. Or the kidneys . . .

THE END

You decide to run! The farther you stay away from that beast, the better. Besides, considering those glowing eyes you saw from the bus, this is obviously no normal wolf.

How do *you* know it can't climb?

You turn to your left and shoot through the trees. Soon you find yourself on a path. You tear down it and glance back. No sign of the beast.

Yes! Maybe you've outrun it!

Then a howl comes from behind. It's close! *Too* close! You put on an extra burst of speed.

That's when your ears pick up a different sound — voices! Uh-oh. What if the teachers from Ranewash have found you? You drop to all fours.

Crawling forward, you peer out onto a clearing in the forest. The path seems to end at the mouth of a dark cave. *That's* where the voices are coming from, you realize.

But who's in there? you wonder. You don't have much time to find out.

Howwwl!

You decide to go into the cave.

Whoever's in there, they can't be worse than the beast!

Crawl to PAGE 39.

You head over to science class.

You take a seat and stare down at the lab table. Whoa! In front of you are some nasty-looking instruments. They include a scalpel, scissors, and a long, sharp tool that looks like it belongs in a dentist's office. What do you need *these* for?

The teacher calls the class to order. She holds up a tiny electronic device between two fingers.

"Today we're going to learn about bugs," she announces. "Not the creepy, crawly kind, but the electronic kind that emit a homing signal."

She picks up another device, about the size of a TV remote control. She flicks it on, and it begins to beep. The beeping gets louder and faster as she moves the remote closer to the bug.

You'd be impressed — if you weren't sure there was something strange going on here.

"Of course, these bugs are also good for keeping track of people," the teacher adds. Then she puts something else on her desk.

You gasp. You can't believe your eyes.

It's a human arm. . . .

Try to stay out of arm's way on PAGE 91.

The door to your room swings open. You tumble through — and shut it tight behind you.

SLAM! You hear the animal smash into the other side of the door. The huge dog howls, a sound that sends shivers up your spine. But soon you hear its snarls fading away.

Whew! It's leaving!

But what are you going to do now?

Then you spot a slip of paper on your bed. It's the one you found when you first arrived! You pick it up and read, RANEWASH BOARDING SCHOOL IS *BRAINWASH* BOARDING SCHOOL.

You shudder. This place is so weird, you get the feeling this isn't a joke.

Then you remember the monocle in your pocket. On a hunch you slip it in front of your eye and take another look at the piece of paper.

Take a glimpse on PAGE 32.

You click on the E-mail program.

The chattering sound of a modem connection comes from the computer. A window to write your E-mail in pops open.

You type in your parents' address and start a letter. . . .

I think something funny is going on here at Ranewash. All the students seem like zombies or something. I found this monocle that shows hidden messages everywhere. It's almost as if they want to program the students. . . .

DING! A message box pops up on your computer:

REPORT TO THE DETENTION WING.

IMMEDIATELY.

Yikes! What you were writing was being monitored! You're caught!

The teacher stands. She puts a firm hand on your shoulder and leads you to the door. Two men in uniform wait outside to "escort" you to the Detention Wing.

Head to PAGE 28.

You vote for Max's plan. Exposing the school by — gulp! — taking pictures of the Detention Wing.

"Good choice!" Max bellows.

Ally grits her teeth and shakes her head. "Well, let's get the cameras ready and go."

Max happily hands out cameras to all of you. You follow behind him as he leads you to a grim building off to the side of the school.

"The Detention Wing," your companions whisper nervously. A few of them glare angrily at you.

You can't believe you voted for this crazy plan!

"Everyone take a window," Max orders.

You all creep up to the building, careful not to make a sound. You peek through a window and gasp at what you see.

The Detention Wing is more like a prison than a school. There are cells and barred windows and even chains on the walls! The rest of the world will *have* to believe you when they see these pictures.

You carefully raise the camera to one eye.

You push the shutter button.... Ahhhhh! Something sprays right into your eye!

Try to see your way to PAGE 57.

"I see you've been using unassigned colors!" the teacher says accusingly.

You gulp. She knows! She knows you were messing with the invisible paint!

"It was just an acc-accident," you stutter.

"You weren't supposed to touch any colors but the ones in the mural. I'm afraid I have to give you fifteen demerits," she concludes.

Uh-oh! If you get twenty-five demerits, it's off to the Detention Wing. Fifteen is more than halfway there!

She takes your class schedule and writes *fifteen demerits* on it with a bright red pen.

The question is, did you already have some other demerits?

Total your demerits. If they add up to twenty-five demerits or more, go to the Detention Wing on PAGE 28.

If they add up to less than twenty-five demerits, write fifteen demerits *on your class list and go to your next class. If you have forgotten the room number, check the list on PAGE 60.*

You and Kate head down the hall toward the front office. You creep past rows of lockers, trying not to make a sound. You pass the office and find yourselves at the open front doors of the school. Yes! Outside at last!

"You're late!" a voice shouts behind you. "Come on!"

Yikes! Who's that? You turn toward the voice.

It's a student who's standing in line in front of the school. The kids in line are boarding a school bus.

It's a field trip, you realize.

You glance quickly at Kate. You can't believe your luck. This is the perfect way to escape!

You board the crowded bus with the other students. You have to sit all the way in the back, one row behind Kate. You spot the teacher at the front of the bus, looking through a monocle. She's checking out all the students.

Checking to see if they're all zombies!

"Duck!" you whisper to Kate. If the teacher doesn't see you, she won't be able to tell you're not a zombie. You scrunch down in your seat.

Too late! The teacher glares directly at Kate. "Just a moment!" she yells.

Oh, no! You're busted.

Turn to PAGE 53.

You decide to try to broadcast a warning to the world. You don't want any more kids to get trapped in Ranewash, the way that you almost did.

You enter the television station. Everyone in the building seems really busy, so it's easy to sneak into the studios.

You peek through one door after another, trying to find out where the news is being broadcast.

Finally, you find a studio labeled NEWSROOM. Inside, you see an anchorperson sitting behind a desk. Bright lights and cameras are pointed at him. "Welcome to *The Five O'Clock News*," the man says into the camera.

Yes! The news! This program must go out live every night to millions of people! It's your perfect chance to tell the world about Ranewash Boarding School!

You sneak through the door, take a deep breath, and bolt in front of the camera!

"I'm a student at Ranewash Boarding School!" you yell into the lens. "And the teachers there are trying to turn everyone into zombies so they can take over the world!"

"Cut!" calls a voice from behind the bright lights.

Uh-oh. Looks like your show is over. . . .

Change the channel to PAGE 131.

You slam down the phone and back away from it. You are now, officially, totally, freaked out.

Just go to the assembly hall, you think. You'll find another way out of here.

You turn toward the assembly hall and come face-to-face with a huge black dog. Its red eyes are just like the eyes you spotted in the forest. It snarls — and you can see its long, sharp fangs.

Your throat seems to close off. You can't swallow. You can hardly breathe.

"N-nice doggy?" you stammer.

"Not a nice doggy." Miss Simms's voice comes from behind you. "A very *mean* doggy." You feel her cold hand on your shoulder.

"I had a feeling it was you who 'borrowed' my monocle," she exclaims. "And now here you are without a hall pass!"

"I was just making a ph-ph —" you stutter.

"Phone calls are not allowed between classes!" she tells you. "I think you need a little trip to the Detention Wing! This *doggy* will take you there."

You have no choice! You walk toward the Detention Wing escorted by the huge dog. Miss Simms's cackling laughter echoes after you down the hall.

Turn to PAGE 28.

You decide to trust Kate and show her the monocle. After all, you can't take on the whole school by yourself.

"I think your story idea is great," you exclaim. "Maybe we could work something like this into it." You thrust the monocle into her hand.

"Just don't let anyone see it," you whisper.

She seems confused for a moment, then holds the monocle up to her eye. First, shock spreads across her face. Then she nods her head, a fierce look in her eyes.

She is silent for a moment.

You shift in your chair nervously, hoping you've made the right choice.

Then Kate raises her hand!

"Excuse me," she calls to the teacher.

Your heart starts to hammer. Is Kate turning you in?

You try to shrink into your chair. Your hands grip the edge of your desk until your knuckles turn white.

Turn to PAGE 40.

Your panicked gaze falls on a poster of George Washington. He's wearing a powdered wig.

"Uhhh — wigs?" you ask.

The teacher sighs. "No, I don't think so. And I thought I wouldn't have to give out any demerits today."

He takes your class schedule and writes *fifteen demerits* on it with a big red pen.

No! you think. Not demerits! The image of the "example" kid you were shown in homeroom flashes into your mind. You can clearly remember his glassy, vacant eyes. If you get twenty-five demerits, you'll go to the Detention Wing — just like him!

The question is, are you headed there right now?

Total your demerits. If they add up to twenty-five demerits or more, go to the Detention Wing on PAGE 28.

If they add up to less than twenty-five demerits, write down fifteen demerits *and go to your next class. If you have forgotten the room number, check the list on PAGE 60.*

"I think we should gain control over the huge dogs that guard the school," Ally says. "The teachers control the dogs with smells. So we snuck into the school and found the bottles of scents they use."

"The problem is," a dark-haired boy named Max interrupts, "we don't know which scent does what."

"We know how *one* scent works," Ally insists. "The dogs don't attack when they smell it. We can *test* the others."

"No way!" Max exclaims. "My plan is to escape to town. There we can tell everyone what's going on here."

"Will anyone believe us?" Ally asks.

"We'll sneak in and take pictures of the Detention Wing first," Max explains. "I took some cameras from a science classroom. With pictures they'll *have* to believe us."

"All right, you've heard both plans," Ally states. "Now — everyone for my plan, raise your hand."

Some of the Runaways raise their hands. Ugh! Just what you were afraid of. Each plan gets six votes. Everyone stares at you, waiting for your decision.

But both plans are crazy! you think. Trying to control killer dogs? Breaking *in* to the Detention Wing? You wish there was another plan. Too bad you can't think of one.

To go with Ally's plan, cast your ballot on PAGE 34.

To go with Max's plan, vote on PAGE 67.

You swallow as you struggle to read the words in reverse. . . .

HIT ME, KICK ME, SHOVE ME!

You try to wipe the words from your forehead. Oh, no! The invisible marker won't wipe off!

You step out into the hall, stunned. Immediately you're shoved against a wall. A group of students gather to torment you.

"Stop!" you shout. "Think for yourselves!"

But they can't. They've been brainwashed by Ranewash.

As you're crunched against a locker, you wonder how long this marker takes to wear off. Probably too long . . .

It looks like you didn't beat Ranewash at its own game, after all.

Because *you're* the one being beaten!

Which makes this . . .

THE END.

One dog opens its mouth. Its long, jagged teeth shine in the sun. It lunges forward and — licks your hand!

The green scent works!

All the dogs yelp happily like little puppies.

"Come on, doggies!" you command, heading for the school.

They follow obediently behind. A few teachers in the hall point at you and shout, "Runaway!" But the dogs turn on them with fearsome growls, and the teachers scamper away.

With the dogs on your side, nothing can stand in your way. You guess you'll be running things from now on.

Maybe you can even deprogram all the brainwashed students to be regular kids again.

After all, who said you can't teach an old dog new tricks!

THE END

It's not hard to find Room 77, a huge gym at one end of the school.

"Suit up!" a man with a whistle shouts.

Hmmm. Must be the coach. You find your way to the locker room and change your clothes. Too bad you're the last one out on the gym floor.

The angry-looking coach glares at you. His muscles ripple under his clothes.

"Get in line!" he growls. You move to the end of a long line of kids. You all follow the coach to an Olympic-size pool. Then the coach pulls out a pair of glasses and scans the class. The way he's staring through them reminds you of Miss Simms and her monocle.

Wait a minute. Do his glasses work like the monocle? you wonder. Does every teacher here have one of these freaky lenses?

The coach walks along the line of nervous students.

"You all must be pretty smart to be in this school," he grumbles. "But being smart isn't everything! You've got to be fit too," he continues. "Or you don't belong here! That's why today we're climbing the Eliminator."

He points up.

Gulp. You can see why it's called "the Eliminator."

Climb to PAGE 114.

Your hands search your pockets.

Oh, no! You haven't got the fare!

"Can I owe you?" you plead with the bus driver.

He snorts and slams the door in your face.

The teachers begin shouting at you through the fence.

"Fifteen demerits for unauthorized use of the soccer field!" one teacher shouts.

"Ten demerits for leaving school property!" another adds.

"And you didn't register for classes!" a third bellows. "That's another five demerits."

Yikes! That's enough demerits to send you to the Detention Wing. But there's still a fence between you and them.

"You haven't caught me yet!" you shout defiantly.

The three teachers stare cruelly through the fence at you. One pulls a remote control from her pocket and points it at the fence. You gulp as a section of fence rolls down to let them through.

One of the teachers grabs you. "Thirty demerits!" she shouts. "Report to the Detention Wing immediately!"

Report to PAGE 28.

"No way!" you shout. "I won't spy on other kids!"

"That's what *you* think." Miss Pierce cackles.

She hands you a new schedule. It says you're spending next period in the library.

The library is calm after this awful day. You can't help overhearing two students whispering to each other.

"This place is really weird," one mutters.

"Yeah," the other answers. "Half the students act like someone replaced their brains with oatmeal!"

You try to ignore them. But something strange starts to happen. Your head starts to ache — badly. Your brain feels like it's about to explode!

You have to make the pain stop! You walk over to the students.

"Hi," you say.

Instantly your head feels better!

The students start talking to you. As they tell you their suspicions about Ranewash, your head starts to hurt again.

You don't want to, but maybe you should turn them in. It may be the only thing that will stop the pain.

What should you do?

To turn in the two students, turn to PAGE 29.
To mind your own business, turn to PAGE 6.

You decide to run. Anything's better than facing that dog-beast again!

You whirl, twisting out of your captors' hands. You run for the entrance of the cave.

"Hey, wait!" A shout comes from behind you.

No way! You bolt to the mouth of the cave and into the light. You crash blindly through the trees. You just hope you're not headed for the school again.

Or toward the dog-beast!

You emerge into a clearing and fall down, exhausted. You've run so much today, you just can't go on.

Then you hear a low growl behind you. . . .

With your heart in your throat, you turn to face the beast.

"Stay!" you order. "Sit! Heel!"

But this dog doesn't look very obedient.

It takes a few steps toward you, saliva dripping from its fangs.

Then it jumps at you!

Take a bite on PAGE 121.

You decide to take the bus. After all, there's no place like home.

And you're not worried about getting the money for your fare. You've got a theory about the citizens of Ranewash, and you're about to test it out. You walk up to someone on the street and say, "Give me bus fare, please!"

"Of course," says the man. He hands you the money.

Yup. It's just as you thought. Ordering zombies around is no problem. All they do is obey.

Soon you're on the bus, and you are out of there!

Yes! You escaped from Ranewash! You're safe! You sit back and enjoy the ride home. The bus even shows a movie that's really interesting.

Too bad you're so tired after your long day. You nod out as you stare at the screen. And soon you're asleep.

The driver wakes you up at your hometown.

"I noticed you missed the end of the movie," she says. "Take the tape so you can see the whole thing."

"Thank you," you answer, trying to wake up all the way.

"And don't forget to show it to your family," she adds.

"Of course," you agree. You'll do what the bus driver says. Because obeying is good. . . .

Uh-oh. You have no choice but to turn to PAGE 124.

There's no way to escape, you decide, g
around the well-guarded room.

"Here!" you cry. The guard points towar
metal door. You walk through the door.

A white-haired woman sits behind a huge d
She peers at you over her glasses. You shudd
Something in her eyes is positively evil!

"I am Miss Pierce. You are here because yo
can't follow the rules!" she begins. "But even students with behavior problems are sometimes . . .
useful. *If* they're smart."

Useful? You wonder what *that* means.

"I am going to give you a test," Miss Pierce announces. "It will consist of one logic problem."

Gulp. You sit down.

"There is a mill with seven corners," she begins.
"In each corner stand three bags. On each bag sit
seven cats. Then the miller and his wife come into
the mill. How many feet are now in the mill?"

"Uh . . ." you stall. What kind of a question is
that? You'll never figure it out.

"Answer the question!" Miss Pierce barks.
"Now!"

If your answer is more than twenty, turn to
PAGE 52.

If your answer is less than twenty, turn to
PAGE 46.

You haven't got a jacket, but you try to climb the fence anyway.

Your hands grip the chain link. You pull yourself up inch by inch. But when you reach the barbed wire at the top, you realize there's no way you can get over it.

Three teachers arrive below. No! You're trapped on the fence. There's nowhere to go!

The teachers shake their heads at you.

"Using an emergency exit when there's no emergency! Running across the soccer field when you're not even on the team!" one exclaims. "Your behavior is *shocking*!"

"That gives me an idea," another teacher says. She pulls a remote control from her pocket and points it at you.

"I've always said they should leave the electricity on in this thing," she proclaims.

Electricity?

Zap your way to PAGE 129.

You decide to search for the hall pass. It's the only chance you've got to stay alive.

You search around in the underbrush, trying to retrace your path. But in your panic you don't remember which way you came from.

You sift through fallen leaves and branches. You even look under a rock. You can't find the hall pass anywhere!

But you do find something. . . .

About four hundred pounds of hungry dog.

Which makes this a really heavy

END.

The rushing current carries you through the tunnel. *Air!* There's no air! You struggle to hold your breath. Your lungs feel as if they're going to explode!

PLOP! You land on the floor of an enormous room. Air! You suck in a huge breath and stagger to your feet.

You're in . . . a huge kitchen. There's someone standing in front of a giant sink. Hey! It's Abigail!

You rush over to her. "Are you okay?" you ask.

She turns to face you and frowns. "I'm fine — for someone who's going to spend the rest of her life cooking and cleaning!"

"What do you mean?" you ask.

"This is where all the food is prepared for Ranewash students," she answers. "And guess who's got to cook all the meals and clean up?"

"You?" you guess.

"And my new assistant," she says. She hands you an apron. "Someone will be in here in a minute to explain, but trust me — this is our punishment for failing gym. So put this on and start washing!"

"B-but . . ." you sputter.

"Look on the bright side," Abigail says. "We've only got to do this for four years — till graduation."

THE END

You decide to head across the soccer field. It's the quickest way off school property.

Someone's already pounding on the door behind you. There's no time to waste!

Wait a minute — you spot a sign posted by the field.

WARNING:
SOCCER PRACTICE ON MON-WED-FRI *ONLY*!
DO NOT ENTER SOCCER FIELD
ON ANY OTHER DAY!

The sign makes you pause for a moment, but then you shake your head. Why do you care about a silly sign? You're running for your life!

Forget the sign, you decide. You hightail it onto the field.

You start to run. . . .

Not so fast, buddy. You can't just ignore the sign. What day of the week is it?

If it's Monday, Wednesday, or Friday, turn to PAGE 35.

In it's any other day of the week, turn to PAGE 92.

Back at the Runaways' cave, everyone seems really happy to have you around.

"Finally!" one of them exclaims. "A new member to break the tie."

"The tie?" you ask.

"Well, we have two plans for destroying *Brainwash* Boarding School," a girl named Ally explains. "And we've always had twelve members. Every time we vote on the two plans, each one gets six votes."

"So we need a new member to break the tie," another Runaway chimes in.

"Guess I'm lucky number thirteen," you mutter.

Great. Your first five minutes as a Runaway and you've got to make an important decision.

Listen up on PAGE 74.

Your breath catches in your throat as Abigail tumbles through the air.

SPLASH! She disappears underwater for a few horrible moments. Where is she? you wonder. Is she okay? Finally Abigail surfaces, sputtering and coughing.

Whew! you think. But your relief doesn't last long. . . .

"Wash out!" the coach screams, blowing his whistle.

The water in the pool starts to bubble. And a giant whirlpool forms in the center!

What's happening?

Abigail shrieks as she's pushed one way and then another by the waves. Then her body is pulled toward the giant whirlpool!

Oh, no! She's being sucked in!

You gulp as she's washed down into a drain at the bottom of the pool. She's gone!

The kid next to you starts to shake. "This place is seriously scary!" he mutters.

"No kidding," you whisper back.

"Next!" the coach shouts.

Whoa! Are you next? Alphabetical order, remember?

If your last name starts with A–M, go to PAGE 117.

If your last name starts with N–Z, go to PAGE 33.

You try to fight against the hands, but they pull you deep into the cave. Another hand clamps over your mouth, muffling your screams.

More hands grasp your arms and legs. You can't move at all.

Your captors are invisible in the darkness of the cave. They turn you around so that you're facing the opening you were just dragged through. . . .

Your heart pounds with terror as a monstrous shape fills the cave mouth. No! It's the huge dog you saw from the bus.

Its red eyes glow in the blackness. It moves slowly into the cave. A low panting noise fills the darkness.

You try to struggle once more, but your captors' hands are too strong. You can't move!

A whimper escapes your lips. And the beast stares straight at you. . . .

Turn to PAGE 61.

You decide to read as fast as you can.

You zip through the book, speed-reading until your eyes start to bug out of your head.

Mmmmm . . . the voice purrs. *Ancient Greek history.*

No! you think in dismay. It's not working!

But what if everyone in the room does the same thing?

"Read as fast as you can!" you shout to the other kids.

The girl next to you looks puzzled for a moment. But then she starts to read furiously. Her eyes scan the words faster and faster. You plunge back into your book.

Slow down! the voice complains. *Too many words at once!*

Yes! It's working!

You start to hear the voices of other students in your head as they read faster. Algebra and chemistry and social studies all echo through your brain.

Their thoughts are leaking over to you! The brain-sucker must be losing control!

"Everyone read like crazy!" you yell.

Nooooo! the brain-sucker protests. *Ahhhhhh-hhh!*

Read PAGE 94.

Your stomach churns as you stare at the arm. Then you realize — it's not real. It's just a plastic model. Whew!

"Some bugs are so small that you can put them anywhere!" the teacher explains happily. "Even under your skin."

Why would you want to do that? you wonder. A strange coldness starts to trickle into your stomach. What sort of science class is this?

"Here at Ranewash Boarding School, we like to keep track of our students," she says. "So today, we will show you how to put a bug into a human arm."

The teacher smiles. "But why use this plastic model? We have so many healthy young specimens right here in class."

She peers around the room. "Any volunteers?"

Volunteers? you think. Is she *kidding*?

No one makes a sound.

"Well, then." The teacher frowns. "I'll just have to pick someone." She pauses. "How about you?"

You open your eyes.

Oh, no! She's pointing at you!

See if you make the cut on PAGE 48.

You're not *supposed* to be here, but you dash frantically across the field.

"Look over there! That way!" you hear voices shout from behind you.

Oh, no! The teachers and students must have broken through the door.

You turn your head to see how close your pursuers are.

But you can't believe your eyes!

They're just standing at the edge of the field, staring at the sign.

They won't disobey it! Whoa! Those hidden messages you saw must have made it impossible for them to break the rules!

You laugh to yourself as you run. They have to obey the rules *all* the time. Even silly rules like when to use the soccer field.

Ha-ha-ha! They'll never catch you!

You glance ahead and skid to a stop. You gasp. You can't believe what you see in front of you!

Take a look on PAGE 112.

You decide to leave the monocle. You've seen enough to know you want out of this school!

You let the monocle drop from your eye. Miss Simms enters just as you reach your seat.

Whew! you think. Made it.

Miss Simms explains that in a few minutes all classes will be headed to the assembly hall. She calls the roll quickly. She tells you to be quiet while you wait for the bell to ring.

You peer around the room. All the students seem normal again! Without the monocle you can't tell the regular students from the zombies.

Then a puzzled sound comes from Miss Simms. She's staring curiously at her monocle, holding it up to the light.

Uh-oh! you think. Does she notice something?

"There seems to be a fingerprint on my monocle," Miss Simms exclaims.

Yikes! That has to be *your* fingerprint!

"Who has been touching my monocle?" she demands.

Put your fingerprints all over PAGE 38.

Pop! The tentacle falls from your head.

You're free! The brain-sucker couldn't take all that information at once.

You glance over at the huge brain-sucker. You realize it's not so huge anymore. It's shrinking!

Oooooo! it cries. Now it looks more like — a medium-sized octopus.

Eeeee! it yells. Whoops. Make that a teeny-tiny octopus?

Ip! it squeaks. It's *gone*.

Which brings this Ranewash adventure to a really tiny, but satisfying,

END.

Finally the chair's humming sputters to a stop. Your straps are released.

"Go ahead," Dr. Ranewash orders. "Take off the helmet."

You quickly obey. After all, obeying is good!

You peer around the room happily. So many people to give you orders. Yay!

Kate looks upset. And she doesn't obey when they order her to sit in the chair. But you help them strap her in.

She'll be happy once the chair fixes her.

"Now, go back to class," Ranewash tells you. "And remember to work very, very hard."

You smile at this order. Work is lots of fun.

And you don't need to worry. You'll have lots of work to do for the rest of your life.

Which makes this . . .

THE HAPPIEST END OF THEM ALL.

You decide to run for it.

You grab the tentacle on your head and pull as hard as you can.

Stop! the brain-sucker's voice screams in your mind.

"No way!" you shout, yanking at the tentacle.

Oh, dear, the brain-sucker thinks. *Not another zombie!*

What does it mean by that? you wonder.

POP! The tentacle finally starts to come loose. *WHOOSH!* What's that sound in your head? You can't think about that now — run!

Wow. Weird, you think. You're walking so slowly and clumsily. You stumble to the door and reach to open it.

Miss Pierce stands on the other side. "Oh, dear. If only you children wouldn't always try to escape like that. Now all your brains have leaked out. Well, back to class with you, I guess."

You stumble back to class. After all, you have to obey. That's all a brainless zombie can do in

THE END.

You decide to follow the map. You can't be too far from the Runaways' secret hideout.

You move quickly, quietly. One wrong turn could take you into the jaws of a hungry beast!

You can still hear one of them stalking you, crunching heavily through the bushes.

You glance down at the map. Finally you've reached the spot where the Runaways' hideout should be. You peer around frantically.

But there's nothing here!

"No!" you whimper. You fall to the ground exhausted. There's nowhere else to go. You hear a growl and see the dark shape only a few yards away.

Yikes!

Then you hear something. . . .

Voices! They're coming from a cave opening. You can just make it out behind a line of bushes. You rise and run toward it.

You burst into a brightly lit cave. Whoa! It's full of kids. They stare at you suspiciously.

You thrust the map toward them. "I-I —" you stutter.

"Welcome to the Runaways!" one of the kids announces.

Get on the welcome wagon on PAGE 87.

You *are* wearing something made of metal!

Yes! you think. Maybe if they put you in the brainwash chair you'll break it. Then Ranewash will think it doesn't work — and you'll still have a fighting chance.

But then you remember the rest of the warning about the metal. DANGER! it said.

Gulp. That probably means danger to *you*. The chair could barbecue your brain or something.

"Which one of you brilliant students wants to be the first to try my new chair?" Dr. Ranewash asks.

You and Kate exchange panicked looks. Neither of you says a word.

"Having trouble deciding?" Dr. Ranewash says in a kindly voice. "Let me help you. I'll flip a coin. Call it and you win." He cackles. "Or lose — as the case may be."

You feel your heart pounding as the coin spins in the air. Dr. Ranewash catches it, closes his hand, and points at you. "Call it," he orders you.

If you call heads, turn to PAGE 125.
If you call tails, turn to PAGE 43.

You try to stand up, but your legs are trembling too hard.

The guard barks your name again. He glares angrily around the room. You shrink down into your seat.

Maybe if you just sit here, he'll call the next name. Then you could try to sneak out somehow. You know you *don't* want to take the Detention Wing test.

But what if you can't get away? If you get caught, you'll be in more trouble than ever!

What should you do?

To take the test, turn to PAGE 81.
To keep quiet and try to escape, go to PAGE 128.

100

You can't believe it! Before you is a row of strange chairs. They look like — *electric* chairs. The kind used to kill people! Each one has straps on the arms and legs, and an ugly black helmet attached to it. And each helmet has a red label that says DANGER! SUBJECT MUST NOT WEAR ANY METAL!

What are these chairs? Why are they here at Ranewash? You're not sure you want to know the answers.

Silently, Kate points toward the back of the closet.

You don't see anything — until Kate hands you the monocle. You peer through it.

Whoa! you think. A hidden door! The words ENTRANCE 17 are written above it.

"Entrance to *what*?" you wonder out loud.

"Let's find out," Kate suggests.

The thought of opening the door sends shivers down your spine. It says *entrance*, not exit. What if you don't like what you find on the other side?

Your only other choice is to leave the closet and head toward the office — but what if you run into that dog again?

To try Entrance 17, go to PAGE 16.
To go back out to the hall, turn to PAGE 69.

"Uh . . . I was just . . ." you stammer.

"I know what you were up to," the art teacher snaps.

It's true! you realize with horror. Her glasses are just like the monocle!

She pulls out a big felt marker and holds your chin firmly with one hand. She writes something on your forehead with quick strokes of the pen. Then she releases you.

"See how you like Ranewash School now!" she cackles.

The bell rings.

Whew! You hurtle out into the hall.

No big deal, you'll just slip into a bathroom and wash off whatever is written on your face.

Then you feel a sudden shove to one side.

"Ow!" you shout. But the boy who shoved you keeps walking.

What's his problem? you wonder.

Then you feel a bonk from behind as someone kicks you. What's going on here?

You push your way through the crowd. Finally you make it into a bathroom and peer at your forehead in the mirror. There's nothing written there!

Then you remember to look through your monocle. . . .

See your way to PAGE 75.

You decide to try the red bottle.

First you and Ally spray the scent from the blue bottle onto your clothes — so the dogs won't attack.

Then you take the red bottle and head toward the school.

Ally crashes through the bushes, making as much noise as possible. Is she crazy? you think. It's almost like she *wants* to get surrounded by a pack of wild beasts!

"What are you doing?" you ask.

"I'm getting the dogs to notice us. We're going to control them. So we want as many dogs as possible!" she explains.

Is she nuts? Even *one* of these horrible dogs is too many, you think. But there's no way out now. Already, glowing red eyes are peering at you from all directions.

"Here, doggies!" Ally calls.

Soon a snarling pack has gathered around you. But the blue scent seems to work. The dogs sniff it and back off.

"Now to test the red scent," Ally announces. She sprays it on herself and then on you.

You gulp as the dogs lift their noses into the air. You hope you chose the right scent.

Then you peer down at your clothes . . . and scream!

Turn to PAGE 18.

You're glad it's time for art class. It's the nicest-sounding class on your schedule.

Room 103 has a long table. Lying on it is a huge, stretched canvas with shapes already penciled in. Sort of like a color-by-numbers set.

The teacher, a woman with a paint-smeared smock and glasses, passes around paints. She orders you all to fill in the canvas. This isn't a very creative art class, you think.

You take another look at the shapes drawn on canvas. Hmmm. Once this painting is done, it will look just like one of those murals in the hall. The kind with the secret messages.

You slyly put your monocle in front of your eye and peer at the canvas. There aren't any hidden messages on the mural yet. Maybe once the paint is applied . . .

You turn and see an open can of paint sitting unused on a low shelf. Whoa! It's bright red. So bright that staring at it makes you dizzy!

You remove the monocle and stare into the can again. Without the monocle, the paint looks perfectly clear.

You feel yourself smile. This gives you a great idea!

You find yourself drawn to PAGE 23.

You fumble with the flare, but it doesn't work. It's a *dud*!

Gulp.

Maybe following orders wasn't such a good idea.

The dog growls and leaps!

Too bad. Like that flare, this ending is a dud!

THE END

You click on the school's database.

Information about the school's founder, Dr. Ranewash, pops onto the screen. It seems he invented a way of using hidden messages to make people think a certain way.

Cool! you think. Just like the hidden messages all around the school — and in the computer! This is fun. Almost as much fun as obeying!

Wait — what was that thought? And why did you think it? Could the computer's hidden messages be working on you? But — you thought you turned them off.

Oh, well, it doesn't matter. You wish you had some work to do. Because work is good.

You raise your hand, and the teacher comes over.

"Could you give me some work, please?" you ask. "Work is good." Funny. That's not how you usually talk.

But the teacher seems to understand. "Why don't you write your parents a letter, telling them how you want to stay here at Ranewash for the next vacation — to do lots and lots of work," she suggests.

You try to shake your head no. But you can't!

Work your way to PAGE 25.

You decide to show the dogs the hall pass. Maybe it will work.

You thrust the crumpled piece of paper toward the lead dog. The beast growls and takes a step forward. Your heart pounds as its sharp teeth come within inches of your shaking hand.

The dog sniffs the pass.

"RUFF!" It barks in your face. You almost jump out of your skin!

As if the bark is a signal, the other two dogs turn and slink away down the hall. The lead dog growls once more, then turns and follows them.

You stare at the hall pass with wonder. It worked! You raise it to your nose and sniff like the dog. You detect a strange scent.

So *that's* how the dogs are controlled — with scents. If you have the right smell, they won't attack!

You continue down the hall, clutching the hall pass to your chest. Following the map carefully you reach the door that leads outside.

You push it open and emerge into the blinding sunlight. . . .

See the light on PAGE 12.

You're right. The stress of being in a new school is getting to you. Because this school is *wacked out*! Your breath catches in your chest as you gaze through the monocle. Through its lens you can see that the murals on either side of the hallway have hidden messages in them. . . .

NEVER THINK FOR YOURSELF!

WORK IS BETTER THAN PLAY!

NEVER BE IN THE HALL WITHOUT A PASS!

You glance quickly through the monocle at the students crowding the hall.

Just like in the classroom, a lot of them have bluish-green skin and glassy eyes — and numbers on their clothes that are invisible without the monocle.

"Playing isn't really that much fun," you hear one numbered student proclaim.

"That's right," another agrees. "Work is much better."

Whoa! you think. They talk just like the slogans on the walls. What's *that* about?

You feel a hand on your shoulder. Gulp!

"What's that you've got there?" a voice asks.

Take a look on PAGE 60.

Your fingers close around some coins.

Yes! You've got just enough!

You spill the money into the driver's coin tray. The driver nods and closes the door.

"Take a seat, please," he orders as the bus lurches into motion.

Whew! you think, heading for a seat.

You settle back for the ride, wondering what to do next.

The bus pulls into town about ten minutes later. A big sign welcomes you:

TOWN OF RANEWASH, POP. 1,280

You gulp when you read the name. This whole *town* is called Ranewash?

Does that mean the people in town are just like the people in Ranewash Boarding School?

Until you find out, you're going to have to be careful here. . . .

Get off the bus on PAGE 27.

You can't even remember the last time you fell off a jungle gym. You're good at this! You *know* you'll make it across!

But the Eliminator feels like it's made of barbed wire!

The rope scrapes and cuts your hands. The pain is horrible! You feel your grip starting to slip.

Yeaaaaaaaaaah!

The class gasps as you tumble toward the water. You roll yourself into a cannonball at the last moment.

But when you hit the pool, it feels like you're hitting concrete. The rush of water fills your ears like a bolt of thunder.

Maybe you can make it to the edge of the pool before you "wash out." You struggle to the surface, gasping and sputtering. But the whirlpool has already started to boil.

The current sucks you toward a dark drain at the bottom of the pool. And you can't escape!

You catch one last glimpse of the gym before the blackness of the drain swallows you. . . .

Wash out to PAGE 85.

You try to write your essay alone, but you can't concentrate, knowing you'll have to face the teacher after class. What does he want to see you about?

The bell rings. You go up to the teacher's desk, handing him your paper.

He glares at you through narrowed eyes.

"If you can't work with other students, you'll never succeed here at Ranewash Boarding School," he scolds.

You nod your head and swallow.

"But since it's your first day, I'll let you off with a warning," he explains.

You sigh with relief.

"A warning and twenty demerits," he adds.

Your head starts to spin. Twenty demerits! If you get twenty-five, you'll go to the Detention Wing!

You remember the "zombie" student you saw in homeroom and shudder. *He* went to the Detention Wing. Whatever happens there is *not* good.

Man! This whole thing is Kate's fault, you think. Maybe you should explain that to the teacher.

Or maybe you should keep quiet and just take the demerits?

To tell the teacher it was Kate's fault, turn to PAGE 26.

To take the twenty demerits quietly, turn to PAGE 113.

Time to go to history class. Too bad this *whole school* isn't history, you think.

Room 111 seems normal enough. Posters of presidents and war heroes cover the walls.

The teacher is an ancient little man with no hair at all. He glares at the class through a pair of thick glasses.

"Today we are going to watch a very important video," he announces. A few students giggle at his squeaky voice.

He peers around the room, trying to see who laughed. The room quiets, but you relax a little. This guy doesn't scare you like some of the other people around here.

The video starts with patriotic music. Familiar faces from the American Revolution fill the screen. But the video is all about stuff you've known since second grade.

You decide to check out the room with your monocle instead of watching.

You sneak the monocle from your pocket and glance through it. There's no hidden messages in the room that you can see. But wait! The video!

As you watch, your jaw starts to drop. . . .

Fast-forward to PAGE 17.

Rising up out of the ground are a dozen dark, mechanical shapes. They look like huge, hulking lawn mowers — with their super-sharp blades exposed.

You swallow as, one by one, the mowers growl into motion.

And they're moving toward you!

Uh-oh! you realize. *This* is why no one wanted to disobey the soccer field rules. The grass gets cut by these monster machines every Tuesday, Thursday, Saturday, and Sunday.

You take a step away, but the lawn mowers form a tight circle around you. Then they start to close in.

Yikes! This gives a new meaning to the words "cutting classes."

THE END

You decide not to tell on Kate.

After all, no one likes a snitch.

The teacher asks you to hand over your class list. On it he writes *twenty demerits* with a big red pen.

Your heart sinks when you read the words.

It's not my fault! you think one last time.

The question is, have you reached twenty-five demerits yet? If you have, you'll be taking a trip to the Detention Wing. . . .

Total your demerits.

If they add up to twenty-five demerits or more, go to the Detention Wing on PAGE 28.

If they add up to less than twenty-five demerits, write down twenty demerits *on the piece of paper with your class list and go to your next class. If you have forgotten the room number, check the list on PAGE 60.*

The Eliminator is a rope far above you, stretched from one end of the gym to the other. It must be forty feet off the ground!

"Of course, we wouldn't want you to get *hurt*," the coach explains. "That's why the Eliminator hangs over the pool. *Most* students who fall will land in the water."

Most? You swallow nervously. What is this guy trying to do — *kill* you?

"Alphabetical order!" the coach shouts. "Abigail Abbey, approach the Eliminator!"

A short girl steps forward timidly. The coach points to a rope ladder at one end of the Eliminator. Abigail climbs it and peers across the gym to the other end.

She grasps the Eliminator with one hand, then the other, and soon is dangling over your head. Abigail continues, hand over hand, reaching the middle of the rope in no time.

Yes! you think. Keep going, Abigail!

But then she slows down. Her hands shake as she reaches forward. Abigail struggles to hold on. But one hand slips from the rope.

Oh, no! you think. She's going to fall!

Land on PAGE 88.

Pick one! you tell yourself.

"Uh, tea?" you stammer.

The teacher raises one eyebrow. "Are you sure?" he asks.

You gulp. But there's no turning back now. You nod.

"Correct!" the teacher announces.

Whew! you think. That was pure luck. Your shoulders slump with relief.

You made it through that one! But maybe next time you should pay more attention. You *don't* want to wind up in the Detention Wing! And you especially don't want to end up like that zombie kid.

Soon the bell rings, and you ready yourself for the next class.

Go to the next class on your schedule.

If you've forgotten the room number, check the list on PAGE 60.

You decide to stay on the bus and escape that way.

The bus empties. After a few minutes the driver starts the engine again.

Great! You just hope he's not taking this thing back to school.

You stay hidden the whole trip, afraid the driver will see you if you stick your head up.

Finally the bus slows and stops. The driver opens the doors and gets off. You wait nervously for a few moments, then raise your head to see where you are.

A big sign is right in front of you.

WELCOME TO RANEWASH
THE FRIENDLY TOWN

This whole *town* is called Ranewash?

Terrific. You just hope the people here are nothing like the ones at school.

Check out the town on PAGE 27.

"You!" the coach points at you. "You're next!"

You swallow hard. Your stomach twists into knots. Are you going to be "washed out" like Abigail?

You wonder where she is now — and what's at the other end of that underwater tunnel?

You walk to the rope ladder and climb, putting more and more distance between you and the gym floor. Don't look down, you coach yourself. Just *don't*.

Then you put your hand out to the Eliminator's main rope. It feels slick, almost greasy. No fair! How are you supposed to hang on to *this*?

You will your hands to grab the rope, even though they're shaking.

Just go for it! you command yourself. You take your feet off the ladder and hang in midair!

Hand over hand, you move along the rope.

Oh! Your hands are getting tired. Your arms feel like they've been stretched a mile long!

Are you going to make it?

That depends. Can you remember the last time you fell off a jungle gym? If you can, go to PAGE 21.

If you can't, turn to PAGE 109.

Making its way through the treetops, coming right at you, is a huge *cat*. It looks something like a panther — that's been weight lifting!

You gulp as it kneads its huge claws on a branch, shredding bark like it was paper. Then it leaps out onto *your* branch! It swipes a big, heavy paw at you.

You climb higher. But soon you run out of branches, and the big cat is right behind you!

You want to tell it to leave you alone, but you're so scared you can't even speak. What's the matter?

Cat got your tongue?

Well, even if it doesn't yet, it will soon. Because for you this is truly . . .

THE END.

You decide to call your parents. You want to get out of here. And you're sure they'll come and get you.

You take a quick look to make sure no teachers are around. "I-I need to make a collect call," you stammer when the operator comes on.

You glance nervously over your shoulder.

"Hello?" your little sister, Maggie, answers.

"Maggie, get Mom," you order.

"Mom's not here," she responds.

"Then get Dad," you implore.

"Dad's not here either," Maggie teases.

"Well, who *is* there?" you growl.

"Me," she tells you. "And the dog. Oh, and the baby-sitter too."

"Listen, Maggie," you say. "Tell Mom and Dad that there's something really weird going on at my school. Okay?"

You don't hear an answer from her. Instead, you hear something that makes your hair stand on end. . . .

Have a listen on PAGE 11.

You've got to get out of here!

You sit and read, trying to figure out what to do.

Maybe you could read really fast. So fast that the brain-sucker can't keep up. Yeah! Like maybe you could clog it up or something.

But what if that just makes it smarter?

Or on the other hand, you could try to yank the tentacle off your head. And run for it!

To clog up the brain-sucker's brain, turn to PAGE 90.

To run for it, run for PAGE 96.

You're frozen in fear as the dog leaps.

Suddenly a burning flare flies out of the bushes. The beast whirls in midair, yelping in fear.

It crashes against you, knocking you flat. But the flare singes its fur. It runs whimpering into the bushes.

Yes! The beast is gone!

The Runaways emerge from the bushes and crowd around you. "Are you okay?" one of them asks. She helps you up.

"I guess so," you tell her.

"You passed the test!" she announces. All the other Runaways cheer, clapping you on the back.

What is she talking about?

"You didn't obey us," she explains. "So you can't be a spy from Ranewash. All the Ranewash zombies *never* disobey a direct order."

"Oh, I get it," you mutter. At least, you sort of get it.

"So now you're an official Runaway!" she proclaims.

Run away to PAGE 87.

122

Time for computer class.

Room 122 is full of brand-new computers — one on each desk. You sit down, and your computer flicks on automatically.

"Whoa! This is sweet!" the girl next to you proclaims.

The teacher clears her throat. "Today we're going to find out how much you know about computers," she announces. "You can use your computer to do anything you want. Surf the Internet, send E-mail, look up information about the school — whatever. So start working."

No problem, you think. You've always had a knack for computers. The girl next to you jumps into her work.

But as you try out the programs, your head starts to feel funny.

You glance around the room. All the other students seem strangely sleepy. Even the girl next to you has slowed down. Her face looks slack and tired.

"Pretty good machines, huh?" you say to her.

"Must work," she murmurs. "Work is important."

Hmmm. Maybe you should take a quick look through your monocle and see what's up. You put the little lens to your eye. . . .

Take a look on PAGE 36.

"Aaah!" you yell.

You turn and run from the vicious-looking dog as fast as you can. You hear its footsteps just behind you.

No! you think. You have to outrun it!

You round a corner and realize that you're in the students' living quarters. You aren't far from your own room! You dart down a side hallway.

Yes! *There's* your room!

You put on an extra burst of speed.

You twist the handle on your door as the huge dog leaps!

Open up on PAGE 65.

124

You clutch the videotape carefully as you walk home.

You still can't quite wake up. Something about that movie on the bus keeps running through your mind.

You walk along, careful to obey all the traffic signs. After all, obeying is good.

Too bad. It looks like the movie on that bus brainwashed you. Just like the people in Ranewash. Now you think the most important thing to obey is the bus driver's suggestion. You have to show this movie to your family, again and again and again. . . .

Until they also know how important it is to obey too.

After all, the family that obeys together, stays together.

THE END

"H-heads," you stammer.

Dr. Ranewash opens his hand, looks at the coin, and smiles. "Heads! That means *you* go first."

"Noooo!" you scream. But you are dragged to the chair. The straps are bound tightly around your wrists and ankles. The helmet is lowered onto your head.

"Now!" Ranewash yells.

The chair starts to hum. You feel electricity crawling across your skin. It feels as if a nest of spiders is walking on you.

"Aaagh!" you yell.

Then the spiders turn to jolts — in your hands, in your legs, in your nose!

The sizzle of electricity starts to gather around the metal you're wearing. It heats the metal, which starts to burn you.

Owww! You're being fried!

KA-BOOM! You're thrown backwards in the seat. It feels as though you've been struck by lightning!

Finally the chair whines down into silence. Did it work? Have you been brainwashed?

You feel hands working to release the straps. The helmet is lifted from your head. . . .

Turn to PAGE 37.

You decide to make a run for it.

You've had enough science for one day!

The teacher lowers the scalpel blade toward your arm.

You thrust your elbow out to knock over the brown glass bottle.

"Aaah!" the teacher shouts, jumping backwards.

"Sorry," you cry, pulling your arm away.

You sprint for the door, yanking it open and darting into the hall.

This school is totally sick, you realize. You've got to get out of here! You run down the long hallway, searching for an exit.

"Grrrrrr." You hear a fearsome growl from behind you.

You turn — and see an awful beast glaring at you.

It's like the huge dog you saw in the forest, you realize. It has glowing red eyes and long fangs. And it's wearing a tag that reads HALL MONITOR in neon letters.

You remember the words of your guide: "Don't get caught in the hall during classes." Gulp. This must be why.

The dog crouches and prepares to pounce on you!

Pounce on PAGE 123.

You decide to climb a tree. You choose a tall, broad oak with plenty of branches. Swinging up to the first branch is hard. But after that, it's as easy as climbing a ladder.

You hear a growl below and peer down nervously.

Yeow! A huge black dog — just like the one you saw from the bus — glares up at you. It paws the base of the tree and snarls.

Whew! You were right! It can't follow you up here.

"What's the matter?" you taunt. "Can't climb a tree?"

Another dog joins it, then another. The huge dogs are a terrifying sight, but you know they can't get you.

"You don't scare me!" you shout defiantly.

Then the dogs start to howl together. But it's not like the howl you heard before. It's a weird, high-pitched cry that you can barely hear.

R-r-r-r-owwww! Their cry is answered.

What was that? you wonder. You stare in the direction of the noise — into the trees. You can just make out another animal approaching.

Uh-oh. This tree is about to get kind of crowded. . . .

Climb your way to PAGE 118.

You keep quiet. No way are you taking that test!

The guard sighs disgustedly and stomps back to the book. He calls the next name.

Yes! you think. It worked!

But how are you going to get out of here? You stand up, pretending to stretch.

The guard's not looking! You head for the Detention Wing exit. Your hand reaches the knob. . . .

But it won't open!

"Your name has not been called!" the guard announces.

Oops! you think. Busted.

"Sit down until you're called," the guard tells you.

"B-b-but —" you stammer.

"Sit down!" he barks.

You sit. And sit, and sit. Because your name is never called again. You only get one chance to take the test in Detention Wing.

Now it looks like you'll be in detention forever! Which makes this . . .

THE WORST END EVER!

"W-wait!" you stammer. You want to climb back down, but your shirt gets tangled in the wire. "I'm sorry I ran on the field. I'm sorry!" you call down.

"It's too late for that," the teacher with the remote control says, shaking her head.

She twists a knob on the remote.

"*Yeeeeow!*" you shriek. Electricity shoots through you.

Whoops! Looks like you're going to get a big *F* on your report card.

F for *fried*.

THE END

You decide to give up the whole idea. You don't want to get caught messing around at Ranewash Boarding School.

Who knows what they would do to you if you got caught?

There has to be another, less obvious way out of here.

As art class ends, you stand at the sink to rinse out your brushes. Then the bell rings, and you're off to the next class.

At least nothing bad happened here in art class. . . .

But as you pass the teacher on the way out, she calls to you, "Come here for a moment, please."

Uh-oh. Maybe you spoke too soon.

Have you painted yourself into a corner?

Find out on PAGE 68.

"Nice try, kid," a man declares as he steps out into the lights. "But, uh, we're not broadcasting right now."

You stare at the clock and get a sinking feeling. It's only four o'clock. *Oh, no!* your mind screams. *The Five O'Clock News* isn't on yet!

"This is just the rehearsal," the man explains.

You gulp. *No one* saw your warning.

"I like your style," the director adds. "You're a lot more entertaining than all these zombies I've got working around here."

"Really?" you answer.

"*Much* better!" he confirms. "How would you like a job?"

That's how you become the youngest anchor-person in the country. Your first news story is an exposé of Ranewash Boarding School. It gets the whole place shut down — and makes you famous!

You run subliminal messages during your broadcasts that will deprogram all of Ranewash's students, past and present.

So, just as you say every night to close your show, "That's good news for everyone!"

THE END

Kate leans closer. "How about this for a story? Some new students arrive at a boarding school. It's a really creepy place. All the kids there seem to be brainwashed."

You swallow and lean even closer.

Whoa! Kate is on the same wavelength as you. At least someone else seems to have noticed that Ranewash Boarding School is totally creepy.

Maybe you should show her the monocle. And show her what it reveals. Then you two could try to find a way out together!

But can you trust her?

What if she's really one of the zombielike students, just trying to trick you?

Maybe you should play it cool and pretend you don't know what she means.

To show Kate the monocle, turn to PAGE 72.
To play it cool, turn to PAGE 49.

Your eyes scan the room wildly.

It can't be! But it is.

Tentacles — like an octopus's — clutch each of the students by the head. The tentacles all lead to the back of the room — where they're attached to a giant, horrible creature! It's covered with scales and has a *huge* head!

You've got to get out of here! You spring to your feet.

But it's too late! A tentacle wraps around your head and forces you back into the chair.

Read to me!

What? There's some kind of voice in your brain!

Read to me about ancient Greek history. . . .

"Let me out of here!" you yell.

No! the voice shouts. *You have to read to me. Or I'll suck your brain dry!*

A dizzying sensation comes over you. The creature wasn't kidding. It's starting to empty your brain!

You open the book and read. The brain-sucking sensation goes away. But as you read the words in the book, you feel them flowing out of your brain. They're flowing straight into the tentacle on your head!

Go to PAGE 120.

You and Kate stare at each other. You feel as if you can practically read her thoughts. This can't be happening! But it is.

The teachers at Ranewash Boarding School are trying to brainwash you and make you their slaves!

"Now we have invented a way to brainwash a student in just a few minutes," the old man continues. "Behold, the Ranewash Brainwash Chair!"

He points at a chair in the corner. It's just like the ones you saw upstairs, except that it's plugged in. A row of red lights blinks on top of the helmet.

"Wonderful, Dr. Ranewash," one of the teachers exclaims. "Now students can graduate on their first day of school!"

Dr. Ranewash? you think. Whoa! This is the guy who runs the whole school! Even he wants to brainwash you!

"Now all we need is a test subject for the device." Dr. Ranewash cackles. "Or two."

"I think we have two volunteers here!" a deep voice announces from behind you.

You and Kate whirl around in shock. And find yourselves facing two burly men in uniforms.

Oh, no! You're caught!

Turn to PAGE 8.

You look up from your brand-new schedule.

"Time to go to class!" several teachers instruct the students.

Fine, you think. Maybe there you can find out more about what's going on.

Turn to the page that corresponds to the room number of your first class. For example, art is in Room 103. If art is your first class, turn to PAGE 103.